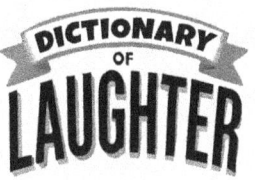

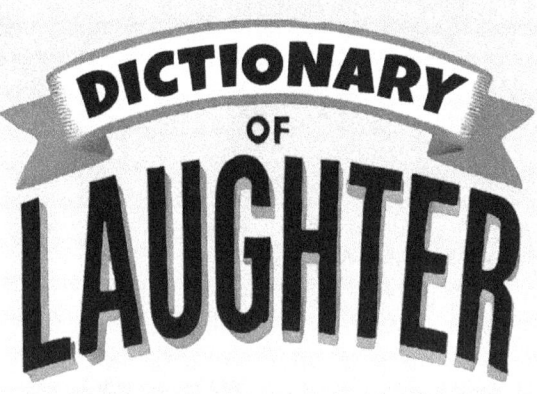

Volume I

never stop Laughing

Ramin

RAMIN ISMAILI

Copyright © 2024 by Ramin Ismaili.

All rights reserved. No part of this publication may be reproduced, distributed, or transmitted in any form or by any electronic or mechanical means, including information storage and retrieval systems, without a prior written permission from the publisher, except by reviewers, who may quote brief passages in a review, and certain other noncommercial uses permitted by the copyright law.

ISBN: 979-8-89228-376-2   (Paperback)
ISBN: 979-8-89228-377-9   (Hardcover)

Printed in the United States of America

This book, *Dictionary of Laughter,* will feature a thousand poems in alphabetical order, presenting poetic debates inspired by people and poets from hundreds of years ago in ancient history. My hope is to make everyone laugh.

Laughter Legacy Press

Your Heart is safe here alphabetically with Love and Laughter

You are going to love what you do, in your life and always have passion for it, otherwise you will quit.

-Steve Jobs

They always said that it's impossible to make everyone happy, but with my *Books of Laughter*, I almost did it—spreading love, joy, mindset, and laughter.

-Be mindful-

A - Amusing Laughter

Always to create
positive vibes in the
world—
that's how galaxies
are made.

Always Laugh From
your Heart
And cry with Laughter—
never with Ego.

Always, my problems
are my Smile.
My Laughter
is contagious.

Always,
Happiness is thinking
about future
with positivity,
gratitude,
and energy—
with Laughter, never Ego.

Always stay with
your magic,
with Love and Laughter.
Then you can say,
"Life is good."

-mindset-

Always, Blessed are
the Hearts that
can Heal themselves
with Love and Laughter

-without closure-

Always in my mind,
I produce positive
Energy to Laugh
a little more each moment—
even with Ego.

Always, in my experience,
People have long
memories.
I hope my Books of Laughter
are contagious
to your Heart and mind,
bringing Lots of Laughter.

All the paths I take
are flown through
every single moment
with Laughter—
and yes, Ego.

All the sources of
Humour come from
Laughing like the Boss,
with a bit of Ego to spare.

Always, I enjoy my Life
with my own Rules—
Rules of Laughter,
like the Boss.
-mindset-

Always Have the Power
to Laugh as Hard as I can
through every moment of my life—
to protect my peace
and Freedom,

Always challenge
Yourself with Love
And Laughter.

Always challenge
Your Brain to see
a productive view,
with Love and Laughter—
because if you want to Be Happy,
It's up to You.

Always make sure
to help people feel positive,
to make them Happy.
Being Positive is a mindset.
We should always
compliment each other,
Lift each other up,
with Love and Laughter.

Always, Laughter,
Self-love,
and self-Respect
are Happiness.

Always,
the most serious things in Life
become funny with Ego—
then laughter strikes.

Always,
with a Good Mood,
Look up at the moon
And stars At night,
with Love and Laughter.

Authenticity Requires
Love and laughter
(with a little Ego)—
when you are Happy enough
with your Life.

Always Remember in Life:
with science gathering
Knowledge (with Ego),
it is faster
than society gathers wisdom—
With Love and Laughter.

Always, I Dreamt
of being Free.
Now I am Free,
With Love,
Laughter,
EGO.

-Happiness strikes-

Always Learn to clap
for others' victories—
With Love and Laughter.

-Your time comes soon-

Always find time for
the things that make me
Feel alive and Happy—
Like the Boss,
with my Ego.

-mindset-

Always laugh
With my magic—
Like the boss,
With ego.

Actually,
Life is Beautiful,
and I Have All the time
to Laugh
For Rest of my Life—
Like the Boss,
with my Happiness,
my IQ,
and my Ego.

Always Feeling Good,
I Feel Free—
With Laughter,
Confidence, and Ego.

Always stand up
for what you think is Right—
with Love and Laughter.
Because usually
You will stand alone.

Always, music is the seed
of Love,
the Language of laughter and dancing—
With Ego.

Always, Love and Laughter
consume most of your time,
Your life—
because happiness
is something
you must create for yourself.

-Mindset-

All the success in Life
Is the Result
of perfect moments
with Laughter.

Any thoughts of Love
And Laughter
Uplift the vibrations
Of the universe.

AGE isn't about,
How old you are,
But young
you Feel—
with Love and Laughter.

Always in my mind,
I Produce Positive Energy
every moment—
with Love and Laughter.

All positive momentum
in life
is magic and laughter—
called Happiness.

Always, there's time
for magic
with Laughter and Ego.

All the success in Life
comes from
perfect moments
with Laughter.

Always, to Be Happy,
you should Look forward
into the future—
with Laughter.

All the sources of Happiness
are Laughter
with Ego.

Always enjoy your Life
with your own Rules—
of Laughter,
with Ego.

Always, Beautiful souls
Recognize Beautiful souls.
Just Keep Being Genuine—
and Laugh
with Ego.

Attitude,
Maturity,
Mindset,
Laughter—
all are Important,
with Ego.

All the sources of
Happiness are Laughter.

B - Belly Laughter

Be you,
and the world
Will adjust.
Love yourself.
Be yourself.

The Best thing about my Life is this:
Every day, I am in transition.
I am replacing
every single thing in my Life
with Something Better—
With Laughter,
Love,
and Ego.

Being Alone is such
a Powerful state,
almost no one can Handle it.
But I do—
with Love and Laughter
When my Ego strikes.

-mindset-

Being calm in Life
is a superpower—
with powered by your IQ
and Ego

Before I speak, I Laugh.
Before I try, I Laugh.
Before I think, I Laugh.
Before I write, I Laugh.
Before I Rest, I Laugh.
Before I work, I Laugh.
Before I spend money, I Laugh.
Because I live
with Laughter.

Being alone holds such
Power that almost no one
Can Handle it.
I trust myself to handle it
with Love and Laughter.

Balance is not free in Life.
You must dance
to the Language of Laughter
to find it—
and keep your Balance
with Ego.

Blessed are the Hearts
that can Heal themselves
with love,
Laughter,
and with Ego.

Without closure,
Build your team so strong
That you can Laugh
with Your Ego,
like the Boss.

Because I always Grow
with my Laughter,
with my IQ,
and my Ego.
-no apologies-

Beautiful eyes
Always search
for the good in others—
with Love and Laughter.

Beauty comes From a Life
Well-Lived.
IF you have Lived well,
your smile Lines
Are in the Right Places.

Be original in Life—
with Love and
Laughter.

Balance is not something
you find.
it is something
you create—
with Love and Laughter.

Behavior is Greater
than Knowledge,
especially when I Laugh
with EGO.

The Body is purified by Water.
The EGO—purified by Laughter.
The Intellect—purified by Knowledge.
The soul—purified by Love.
Tis called Happiness.

Being calm in Life,
with Laughter and Ego,
is a superpower.

Being solid with Laughter
and Ego
never comes
with Instructions.

Being alone
with Ego and Laughter—
so powerful.

Being yourself
is not selfish.
Always Laugh
with your Ego.

Be like the Earth.
When the Rain comes,
the Earth opens up
and soaks it All in.

Because all the superheroes
are cartoons—
imaginary.

Be you,
and the world will always adjust.
Love yourself
with a smile
on your Face.

C - Contagious Laughter

Charlie Chaplin said:
"Life is tragedy in close-up
and comedy from a long shot."
If you sit Back
and view the situation,
everything
automatically gets funnier.
But I am Happy Both Ways.

-mindset-

Choose carefully—
Surround yourself
with contagious energy,
Like Love and Laughter.
Then your Environment
Becomes you—
with Ego.

Confidence,
Built on belief
and self-respect,
is priceless.

Courage
is the magic
That turns Dreams
into Reality.

Collective thinking
Builds Empires—
with powerful Laughter
and Love.

Courage with Laughter
is magic
that turns Dreams
into Reality.

Creativity
is Intelligence
Having fun—
with Love and Laughter.

Creative people
always Laugh
with Ego.

Creative people
always Laugh
Like the Boss—
with Ego.

Confidence,
A Smile,
And Happiness—
They are the prettiest with Ego.

Confidence,
built on belief
and Laughter,
is priceless.

Coffee in one Hand,
Ambition in the other,
and Laughter on my face—
with EGO.

D - Delightful Laughter

Define mindset in one word be mindful.

Define mindful in one word.

Define love in one word.

Define in time in one word.

Define knowledge in one word.

Define peace in one word.

Define ego in one word.

Define world in one word.

Define art in one word.

Define music in one word.

Define coffee in one word.

Define jokes in one word.

Define happiness in one word.

Define laughter in one word.

Dreams are seeds
of your Reality.
Plant them in your Heart,
then watch them grow—
with Love and Laughter.

E - Energetic Laughter

Every day in the future
is a new Beginning—
with Love, Laughter,
and my Ego.

Everything Beautiful
is around you.
Because Beauty starts
in your mind—
With Laughter.

Every smile tells a story,
And my Laughter
changes the world.
Energy speaks Louder
than words.
It's always Like my magic—
the magic of Laughter.

Every time I wish
with my Ego,
Laughter strikes.

Everything you are
Smart enough to imagine.

-is Real-

Every time I wish
with My Ego,
Laughter strikes.

Everything:
Rest,
Nature,
Books—
all flow with laughter.

Every time that I Laugh,
I Laugh Harder,
and then Hardest—
to light up the world.

Every moment of my Life,
I control my mind
to Laugh a Little faster,
to translate
every Language Faster—
With Laughter and Ego.

-Be mindful-

Every day in the future
is a new Beginning—
with Love, Laughter,
and my Ego.

Everything Has a spirit;
Honor that
with Love and Laughter.

Every day,
your Laughter
changes the world.
I never let the world
change my smile.

Exist on your own Terms,
with the Language of Love
and Laughter—
with Ego.

Everyone has
A different clock.
Wait for your own time—
with Love and Laughter.

Encourage with Laughter
that's wealth.
Courage and ego
Go hand in hand.

Every smile
tells a story—
with Ego.

Every Emotion I feel
Right now is valid.
My only Emotions are
Laughing—
with Ego.

Every day is International
Day of Laughter
All around the World.

Every day, your Laughter
changes the world.
I will never let the world
change your smile.

Every next moment,
I burn too Brightly,
collapsing into myself
with laughter,
with love,
with joy,
with happiness,
with ego.
That's How Galaxies
are made.

Empower the one's you Adore—
to take flight with wings to soar,
to establish Roots to stay,
to find strength in reasons to remain—
with love and Laughter.

Embrace Life's Elegance,
and let your Journey
inspire the world—
with Love and Laughter.

F - Friendly Laughter

Failure and success
are only illusions.
Just Laugh
and live in the moment.

First, you Dream
with Ego.
Then, you Laugh—
Like the Boss.

Fear is a Joke—
with Love, Laughter,
and Ego.

Forever, I am obsessed
with sunsets, flowers, the moon, the sun,
Earth, the universe, nature, galaxies
and stars.
Because with Laughter
In my Heart and Soul,
I can fly around the universe.

-that's called mindset-

Fear only Exists
in your mind.
That's why I Laugh
like the Boss—
with Ego.

Fear only Exists
in your mind
that's why I Laugh so much
with my Ego.

Fashion is the perfect
pleasure to survive
the Reality of everyday Life—
with confidence,
Love,
and Laughter.

G - Genuine Laughter

Good Morning—
may your Heart Be Blessed,
and may your life
Be filled with happiness,
Love,
and Laughter.

God often whispers
To gentle Hearts,
with Love and Laughter.

God is often found
Gently whispering
In the Quietness
of a Humbled Heart and Soul,
with Love and Laughter.

Gratitude and Good moods
Make you fall in Love
With your Life.
That's why I laugh
every moment of my life—
To make my memories
Unforgettable,
like a boss.

God is often found,
Gently whispering
In the Quietness
of a Humbled Heart and Soul,
with Love and Laughter.

Greatness is not a skill—
It's an attitude,
with Laughter
and Ego.

Galaxies reside
in my Laughter,
each second of my life.
Even when I translate
all the Languages.
I do it
with Laughter and ego—
like the Boss.
The greatest thing in Life
is learning How to Love
with Laughter
And Ego—
like the Boss.

Gratitude and
A Good Mood
make you fall in Love
with your Life.
That's why I Laugh
in every Moments—
To make my memories
Unforgettable,
like the Boss.

GRATITUDE AND GOOD MOOD
MAKE YOU
FALL IN LOVE WITH YOUR LIFE

Greatness is not a skill—
it's an Attitude,
Built with Laughter
and Ego.

Growth sometimes means
you have to Laugh endlessly—
with your Ego.
The greatest satisfaction
and pleasure in Life
Come from doing
what people say
you cannot do.
Just Do it—
with your Laughter and Ego.

Galaxies reside
in the Laughter
Of each second
of your Life.
Even as I Translate
All the Languages,
It is done
with Love and
Laughter.
A good sense of Humor,
A dirty mind,
And a Beautiful Heart—
together,
are a Deadly combination
with Laughter.

H - Happiness Laughter

Happiness is thinking
about the future—
with positivity, gratitude,
and energy,
with Love and Laughter.

-Happiness is mindset-

Happiness is not a place.
It is a mindset of Laughter—
spreading all around the world
and universe.

Happy Beginning of summer
with a perfect sun,
clear skies,
the moon,
and stars,
wrapped in love
and Laughter.

Honestly is a very Expensive gift.
Don't expect it
from cheap people.
Life is Love
and Laughter.

Happiness is Dancing
under the sunset,
the moon,
and stars—
with Ego,
like the Boss.

Happiness is All about
Laughing as much as you want.

-Love your Life-

Have the sense
to ignore the nonsense—
with laughter
and Ego.

Happiness, confidence,
and smiles
are the prettiest things
you can wear—
with Ego.

The Higher I succeed,
the smarter I appear
to those who cannot fly
with their Imaginations—
Like the Boss.

Happiness is a choice,
not the Result
of Love and Laughter.

Happiness,
with Love and Laughter,
is always FREE.

How to stop time: Kiss.

How to spend time: Read.

How to escape time: listen to music.

How to feel time: Write.

How to Release time: Breath.

How to enjoy time: Laugh.

Health is not
just Physical.
It Includes peace of mind,
peace of Heart,
And peace in your soul—
with Lots of Love
and Laughter.

Happiness always Free—
with Laughter and Ego.

Happiness is All about
Laughing as much as you want—
with your Ego.

Happiness,
with Laughter,
is Dancing under the sunset,
the moon,
and stars—
with Ego.

Happiness is not a place.
It is a mindset—
with Love and Laughter.

Hope,
is the Ability to Hear
the music of the future.
Faith
is Having the courage
to Dance to it today—
with Love and Laughter.

I - Infectious Laughter

If you have passion
for something in life,
you go to extremes
to understand it
and get it right—
With the Language of Laughter
and Ego.

I continue to work
to make everyone Happy
with my Books of Laughter,
Because I have never worked
A single day in my Life.
My Life has always been joyful,
With a positive mindset.
Be mindful.

If you want to Be Happy,
It is up to you.
Live your Life.
Live your Dreams.
Always Laugh.

I want to show everyone
that it is possible
to be Happy
and successful in Life—
with Laughter
and ego.

It is the magic of our laughter
that helps us discover
wings we never knew we Had.

I am Ready to Laugh
All my Life—
with Ego.
Are you Ready?

In this Beautiful world
I trust love
to Wake me each morning
With a smile
on my Face.

I am smiling today,
I was smiling yesterday,
And I will smile tomorrow.
My future is All smiles.

I never take Life Seriously,
Because I am always Busy
Laughing at the future.

I never regard my work
As Duty,
But As an Enviable opportunity
to explore the liberating beauty
of my Intellect—
for personal Joy and music,
like the Boss.

I have never known Darkness
In my Life,
Because of the Illumination
from the Guiding light
of my own Heart and Soul—
filled with Love,
Joy,
and Laughter.

In a sense,
trust is simply
a stronger, more grounded
version of faith—
with Love and Laughter.

I usually don't stay
Where I am simply needed in Life;
I stay where I am valued—
Where I find Love and Respect,
with Love and Laughter.
The greatest thing In Life
is learning how to Love—
with laughter,
Like the Boss.

I Love falling asleep
to the Sound of Rain,
Like the gentle miracles
of mother nature.

If you cannot Handle Stress
with Laughter,
You cannot Handle success
with Ego.

I always Laugh
At superheroes in cartoons and movies—
Because All superheroes
are Imaginary.

I Deserve to Be a Priority
Because I Have the option
to Laugh—
with my Ego.

I always have the power
to laugh as hard as I can,
every moment of my Life—
to protect my peace
and freedom.

I Became
what I choose to Become
with Ego
and Laughter.

I am always me—
The Boss.
The world will adjust
accordingly.

I Have a Beautiful Heart,
with Ego—
And that's Rare.

I Love Life—
With my Ego.

I usually forget
Those who forgets me—
With Ego
and Laughter.

I know the value
of every single moment
In my life,
Because I have been Laughing
For the last 62 years—
Like the Boss.

I always feel good.
I always feel free—
With laughter,
Confidence,
And ego.

I have no obligation
To remain the same person
I was even one second ago,
Because I am always growing—
with my Laughter,
my IQ,
and my Ego.

-no apologies-

Every morning:
Coffee first,
then I Rule the world—
Like the Boss,
with Lots of Ego.

I always Laugh with
my magic—
Like the Boss
with Ego.

I know who is fake
And who is Real.
I just enjoy watching
Their Acting skills—
and Laughing,
like the Boss,
with the Hugest Ego.

I love what I do
I do what I love
I love to laugh

I trust the vibes
from my Laughter Reactions.
That's my mindset—
Like the Boss.

I live a simple Life,
where every day brings Perfection,
fueled by my Laughter
and Ego.

I create light
with my own magic—
with Laughter,
like the Boss.

I am falling in Love
with taking care of Myself—
Like the Boss,
with Ego.

I always find time
for the things that make me happy,
That make me feel alive—
Like the boss,
With my ego.

-mindset-

If you are Lucky enough
to Be Different,
never change.
Be you—
Like the Boss,
with Ego.

I alone Hold the key
to the combinations of the world—
with my Heart,
Because I am the Boss,
with Ego.

I Admire those
who carry Inner peace—
like the Boss,
with Ego.

I Don't Believe in Age.
I Believe in the energy
of Laughter,
Of magic,
and of endless translations—
all with Ego.

Imagination is Far more important
than Knowledge.
My Imagination is magic,
translating every Language
with Laughter and Ego.

I have simple tastes in Life.
My magic is perfectly magical—
Yes, always perfection.
I can Buy Love—
Because when Love is Real,
It's priceless.

I always dreamed of being free.
Now I am free—
with love and ego.
Happiness strikes.

In Life,
it is what it is—
Laughter and Ego,
when you Laugh All Day.

I am always me—
the Boss.
And the world
will Adjust,
Accordingly.

I enjoy my Life,
Living by my own Rules—
of Laughter,
like the Boss.

I have the power
To see life my way—
With Laughter
And my world-class jokes.

I deserve to be a priority,
Because I have the power
to kill you with kindness,
With Laughter,
and my first-class jokes.

If you hate someone
more successful than you,
You have already been Defeated—
by their Laughter
and Ego.

Success isn't free.
You'll only find it
in the dictionary.
But happiness and laughter?
Those are free—
Like the Boss.

-Dictionary of Laughter

I have fun
with my Happiness,
My Laughter,
The Joy of Life,
My world-class jokes,
My self-love,
Respect,
Love,
And Music—
All With Love and laughter,
Like the Boss.

If you sacrifice your Life
with Love and and Laughter,
Love Begins.

I just choose to Become
What I am—
with Love,
Laughter,
And a touch of Ego.

I know who I am
Because I gave myself permission—
with Love, Laughter,
and a Huge Ego.

If you have Graduated
From the best university
but Don't know what's going on
Around you,
you know nothing.

I create my own Life:
my own Heart,
my own peace,
my own Joy,
my own perspective,
my own truth,
my own Art,
my own story,
my own world,
my won Ego—
my Amazing Life.
Like the Boss.

I am not like everyone else.
I am definitely original.
I am me—
with Ego.

If you ever fall in Love,
you feel it Inside
and Laugh outside—
with Ego.

I can Buy Love
with Laughter—
Because when the Love is Real,
it is priceless.

I Love my Ego.
It is self-respect,
wrapped in Laughter.

I Love what I Do.
I Do what I Love.
I Love to Laugh.

Imperfection,
with Love and Laughter,
is called Freedom

I Built a team so strong,
everyone knows—
I am the Boss,
with Love and Laughter.

I always keep my Life simple—
perfection
with Love and Laughter.

I Have no obligation
To remain the same person
I was one second ago.
I am always growing—
with Laughter
and Ego.

I always find time
For the things
that make me Laugh—
with Ego.

I laugh 24/7—
hiding my Happiness.

In Life:

30 Days of Happiness

720 Hours of Good Health

43,200 minutes of Blessings

2,592,000 seconds of Laughter

all with EGO.

I Admire those
with inner peace—
Like Laughing machines
with Ego.

I teach everyone
How to Laugh—
with Ego.

I always face Life
with my first-edition jokes,
Lots of Laughter,
and Ego.

I always trust vibes
when I am Laughing—
with my EGO.

If Life makes you Happy,
then Laugh—
with Ego.

I never take Life seriously.
I am always too Busy Laughing—
with my Ego.

Intelligence,
Positive Energy,
Confidence,
And a smile with ego—
Are the sexiest Habits in Life.

I am kind to my Mind—
like magic.
That's why I laugh so much,
with my Ego.

In Life,
If you don't Have something
money can't Buy,
then you Have nothing.
Respect, manners, morals,
Character, trust, patience,
Class, Integrity, Love,
common sense, Health—
these are priceless,
with Laughter and Ego.

I never Regret anything in Life.
I always get what I want—
with my Ego.

I always face Life with a smile
until my stomach Hurts—
with my Ego.

If you want to succeed
with your own Ideas,
you must Do it alone—
with your Laughter
and Ego.

I never SEEK
validation from anyone.
My Ego approves my Life.

I am the only magician
in the world—
Because I Laugh
with my EGO.

I am only Responsible
for what I say—
not for what you understand—
with my Ego.

I always talk to people
who make me see the world
Differently—
with love and Laughter.

I always solve everything
in the world
with Love
and Happiness.

I love what the sun
Does to me—
with love and Laughter.

I always sing
my own songs—
with Laughter.

I Don't Believe In Age.
I Believe in the energy
of Laughter,
magic,
and EGO.

I Dance with music,
Laugh with my magic,
and always laugh
with my music.

I Love falling asleep
with Laughter,
especially when it is Raining—
Like music.

It's a multiple-cup-of-coffee
kind of day—
with Love and Laughter.

I Love the smell
of warm coffee,
Bloomed Roses,
and new Beginnings—
with Love and Laughter.

I Love my coffee
every single morning.
I call it Happiness —
and it makes me Laugh.

I always Laugh
During Breakfast with coffee—
my stomach Aches,
But it helps me Digest my Food
with my EGO.

In this Beautiful World,
I love waking up each morning
with coffee
and Laughter.

I HAVE THE POWER
TO LOOK AT EVERYTHING IN LIFE
MY WAY—
WITH LAUGHTER
AND MY WORLD-CLASS JOKES.

I always Laugh
with my first-class Jokes—
and my Ego.

J - Joyful Laughter

Just pick any Language,
and I will translate it
into the universal Language
of Laughter—
with Ego.

Just Because I carry Life so well,
making it look easy with my magical Touch,
my Laughter,
and my Ego,
doesn't mean it isn't Heavy.

Jealousy and stupidity
are the same.
(Just Laugh)

Judge me when
you are perfect—
Because I am Laughing Anyway.

Joy is what Happens
when we Recognize
How Beautiful the world is—
with Love
and Laughter.

K - Kindhearted Laughter

KIDS like to cry,
Men like to smile,
Bosses like to Laugh.

Knowledge is not Free—
you Have to pay Attention
with All your effort,
Your money,
and your Laughter.

L - Loud Laughter

Lets go beyond this World
with this Book of Laughter,
Arranged Alphabetically.

Life is great—
With Love,
Laughter,
with Ego.

Live out of your Imagination—
with Laughter,
like the Boss.

Life is a one-time offer,
Which is why I always Laugh—
with Ego.

-mindset-

Life is not measured
By the number of Breaths we take,
But By the moments
That take our Breath Away—
with Love and Laughter.

Life of the Boss—
With my IQ and Ego.
Dance.
Music.
Laugh.
Love.
Jokes.
Magic.
Ego—
With my Happiness,
I cannot stop Laughing.

-mindset-

Life is one-time Offer—
That's why I always laugh
with ego.

-mindset

Life is a circle of Happiness,
Laughter,
and Good times.

Let's cuddle on a Rainy day
and watch old movies—
with Love and Laughter.

Life is always moving.
I am always celebrating
Optimism, Love, Hope,
and Life itself—
through my Laughter,
my smiles,
And amazing memories.

-cheers to Life-

Love is never Boring.
It teaches the Importance
of Self-respect
and Self-love—
With Ego.

Love and Laughter—
A perfect combo of Happiness—
with Ego,
like the Boss.
233

Creativity is a Response
to Laughter—
with Ego,
like the boss.

Life is too short
to be normal.
that's why I cannot stop Laughing—
with Ego.

Laughing with originality
Is more valuable
than Succeeding with Imitation.
It allows for Self-expression
And showcases
a unique Perspective.

*Life with Laughter is very simple,
rooted in my Deepest understanding.

-Life is perfect-

Less Expectation,
more Love—
with Laughter.

Long-term success
is All about
Vision,
Innovation,
Organization—
with Love and Laughter.

Love All,
trust no one,
always Laugh.

Laughter always
fills the Air
with Love.

Love with Laughter
also teaches you
the importance of
self-Love,
self-Respect.

Love with Laughter
is a splendid thing,
Just like the Love songs
say.

Love and Laughter
Together
is Happiness.

Love is Just a word
until someone like me
comes along
and gives it
meaning with Laughter.

Love starts
with smiles,
grows with a kiss,
continues with Laughter.

Logic is the foundation
of certainty;
with Love and Laughter,
we Acquire
every single moment
with Ego.

Live out of your
Imaginations—
with Love and Laughter.

Life is All about
what you made of it,
with Love and Laughter,
not circumstances.

Life is not about
Breathing Air
every moment of your Life.
Life is about moments
When someone
takes your Breath away
with Love and Laughter.
Breath like the Boss,
with Ego.

Life is All about
what you make of it—
with Love and Laughter,
not circumstances.

Live out your Imagination
with Laughter and Ego.

Life is like Riding a Bicycle—
to Keep your Balance,
you have to Keep Moving—
with your Ego.

Laughter is Like
A remote control—
always controlling
the world
with Ego.

Life is not
a perfect storm;
it is perfect Happiness
with Love and Laughter,
and the umbrella
is my Faith,
protecting my Peace.

Laughter is not
an Attitude;
it is Art.
I am an Artist with EGO.

Life is All about
smiles and Laughter

Life is a circle of:
Happiness
Laughter
Good times
music
with EGO

M - Mindful Laughter

My smile is the curve
which can make so many things
Straight.

My favorite kind of Laughter
is when I laugh so hard
That I am in physically pain—
when people truly Appreciate
my Jokes.

My hugest ego
Is built on self-respect and success,
The foundation of my successful life
and my future.

-I am the boss

Music keeps me alive—
with Dance moves,
Ego, Love,
and Laughter.

Mindset is everything In Life.
That's why I Laugh so much
from my Heart and soul with Ego.

My universe is calm and
Peaceful—
that's Equals Happiness for me.
As the Boss,
there's always time
for more Laughter.

Music is Equals Happiness.
It is that simple.

Music is the one Language
we all speak.
Music is life.
Music is Love and Happiness.

Music is peace.
Music is life.
Music is Love and Joy—
Joyfully for the Boss,
with Ego.

Music is a miracle,
striking Happiness
with Laughter and Ego.

Mindset is everything in Life.

-Just Laugh-

The magic of Love
is Found in kisses and Hugs,
wrapped in translations.

Music in the soul
is Heard by the Universe—
with Laughter.

-Life is Good-

My Intelligence
Is my Action
and my good mood,
Because I laugh so much—
like the Boss.

My way of joking
is to laugh
and tell the truth.
That's why my jokes
are the funniest
in the world.

My Knowledge
and good character
Earn me Respect and power—
Like the Boss.

My world-class jokes,
My self-love,
Respect,
Love,
And Music—
All come With Love
and laughter.
Like the Boss.

My Happiness is free—
And that's the most Logical
Explanation,
like the Boss,
with my Hugest Ego.

My smile is the curve
that straightens so much—
with ego.

The most Important thing
in Life
is a fewer negative Thoughts,
more positive Knowledge,
and Laughter—
with Ego.

Music is a war
against My Laughter.

Music is the Art
of thinking
with sounds.

Music is Life
with Laughter.

Music is what feelings
Sound Like—
the sounds of Laughter.

My Happiness
is Beyond Greatness—
with Laughter.

My Intelligence
is my Action
always fueled
by Good moods,
Because I laugh so much—
with Ego.

My self-Love
and self-Respect mean
knowing my worth.
I don't need anyone else
to validate my Laughter—
with my greatest Ego.

My weekends
are always
Days of Love and Laughter.

Mindset is everything in Life.
That's why I Laugh so much—
with my EGO.

My funny story
about Laughter and Ego
is that when I start Laughing,
some people get Jealous
for no Reasons.

Maturity is when,
you React with Laughter,
then walk away—
with your Best Dance moves.

My fighting skills
are laughter—
with my Ego.

My Ego is Important—
Like—
self-Respect,
self-Love,
and my Laughter.

My Motto is very Simple:
I always Laugh—
with my Ego.

A Maestro at work
never looks back,
and everything
follows His Lead.

Music is the Art of
thinking with sounds—
with Laughter
and EGO.

Music is miracle,
when Happiness strikes—
with Laughter and EGO.

Music in the soul
is Heard by the Universe—
with Laughter.

Music with Laughter
Equals Happiness.
it's that simple.

Music is what Feelings
sound Like—
Like the sounds of Laughter.

Music produces
a kind of pleasure
that Human nature
cannot live without—
with Laughter.

Music is contagious
in Heart,
spreading Dancing
and Laughter.

Music sounds
like Laughter.

My way of Joking
is to laugh
and tell the truth.
That's why my jokes
are the funniest jokes
in the world.

Probably, you all need more Oxygen of laughter,
A spark to ignite the joy hereafter.
The letters will continue, the laughter will too,
Stay tuned—Volume Two is waiting for you!

Laughter continues...

www.ingramcontent.com/pod-product-compliance
Lightning Source LLC
La Vergne TN
LVHW090324221224
799603LV00001B/5